D1540334

13
TERRIFYING TALES
From the North Carolina Piedmont

TERRIFYING TALES

From the North Carolina Piedmont

LORIMER PRESS

DAVIDSON, NC

2007

FIRST EDITION
Published by Lorimer Press, Davidson, NC

Printed in China

LIBRARY OF CONGRESS CONTROL NUMBER: 2007929140
ISBN 978-0-9789342-0-0

13
TERRIFYING TALES

∎

Table of Contents

■

> *"They [ghosts] are not actually alive in us; but there they are
> dormant, all the same, and we can never be rid of them."*
> —Henrik Ibsen, GHOSTS

Perhaps this explains our fascination with ghost stories:
we each have the makings of our own ghost within us.
And, if we wonder what awaits us after death, ghost
stories offer one path toward knowing—a glimpse into
our future.

About seventeen years ago, in front of a campfire up
on the Blue Ridge, I had my first encounter with a
Carolina ghost story. Since then, I've enjoyed many other
scary tales, some mountain myths, others populated with
pirates and other scurvy characters that hail from the
coast. But, living where I do, a little north of Charlotte,
two hours east of the mountains, and twice that far from
the ocean, I rarely encounter stories that feature
Piedmont poltergeists, spirits or mythical creatures.

Not in print, anyway.

In 2005, while gathering research for the Town of
Cornelius' centennial, I was surprised to discover one
Piedmont ghost story after another. People swore that
planters still stalk the halls of old plantation houses.
Teachers recalled their terror at the haunted Ag Building
on Catawba Avenue. A chair in Caldwell Station rocks on
a deserted porch. The ghostly outline of a building long
ago burned to the ground reappears each August. And, of
course, accounts of the Loch Norman Monster circulate
among the towns that border our man-made lake. Three
of these stories are included in *A Town By Any Other Name,
A History of Cornelius, N.C.*

That left a lot of good ghost stories unwritten. Or, at least, unpublished.

In addition to an abundance of ghost stories, we have a wealth of good storytellers, too. The combination of which led to this anthology.

. . .

Do ghost stories have to be real? Interesting question.

After announcing our "Call for Entries," we fielded more than one call from prospective contributors wondering if their submission had to be an account of something that had actually happened. Fiction or non-?

Some would argue that "ghost" stories can never be anything but fiction.

But, as Elmer Horton suggests in *Ghosts of Old Winston*, just because we can't explain something, doesn't mean it isn't true. The stories that rang true—whose authors believed them to be true—were, nine times out of ten, the pieces that felt right for this collection.

Woven into these 13 tales are haunted roads, mysterious lights, strange sightings, and a lingering curse. The storytellers include: an English professor from Davidson College, a Charlotte bartender, a house painter, a former police officer from Ventura County, California, several business owners, and a sprinkling of students.

Surprisingly, not all these stories take place in the dead of night. Both Larry Paul and Peterson write about Uncle Ed, whose ghost makes his presence felt at all hours of the day. Robert Troutman Brawley writes of the gentle spirit of Old Ben who appears at the crack of dawn. We have youthful memories from Larry Douglas Starnes and Jeff L. Shook and mid-life musings from poet and author Joyce Marie Sheldon. For animal lovers, there are a couple of dogs (one frisky and one savage), a fateful cat that lures lost drivers off the road, and a flock of vultures.

The Blue Ridge storyteller's words are lost to my memory—I recall only the wonderful combination of cool evening air and crackling fire, and the willingness of every camper to go where the storyteller led us. So huddle up with a few friends, light a fire if you can, and settle in for some chilling tales.

—Leslie Rindoks
editor, Lorimer Press

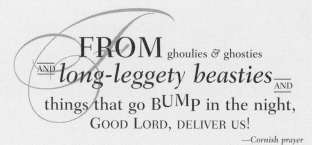

FROM ghoulies & ghosties AND long-leggety beasties AND things that go BUMP in the night, GOOD LORD, DELIVER US!

—Cornish prayer

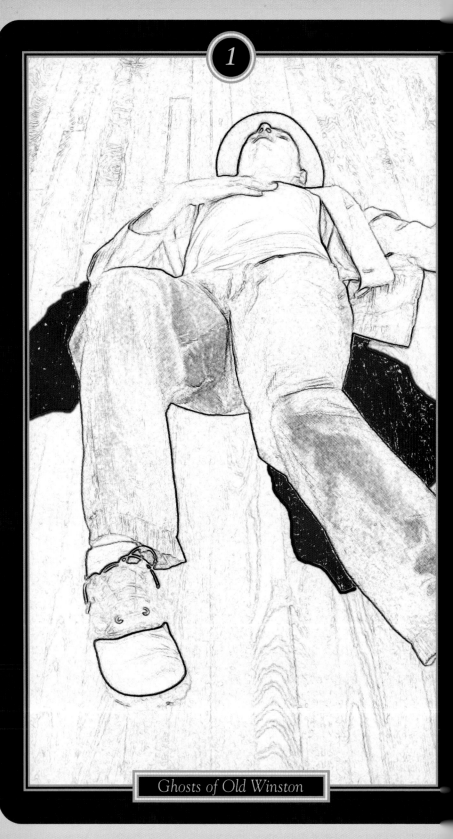

1

Ghosts of Old Winston

GHOSTS OF OLD WINSTON

Elmer L. Horton

■

ALL OF US have heard some spooky stories—but are they real or just figments of our imaginations? I suspect the answer lies in whether you have ever had something out of the ordinary happen to *you*.

As a young boy I listened to my father tell his scary tales. Though there was always doubt in my mind as to whether or not they were true, I knew Dad never had any doubt.

If we can't explain something, does that mean it never happened?

With that in mind, let me share a couple stories I heard from my father—events that happened to him which he couldn't explain, and I'm not even going to try.

• • •

As a young man, my dad moved to Winston-Salem and needed a place to stay. His brother (my uncle) had already moved to town, and was renting a room over a grocery store on Cleveland Avenue. The landlord offered my dad the other second floor room, adjacent to my uncle's.

There was a slight problem; the landlord had only one door key.

Dad decided to take the room anyway.

Every night, around bedtime, my uncle would lock my dad's door from the outside, return to his own room and lock his door from the inside. One night, something roused my dad from a sound sleep. From his bed, he could see a man lying on the floor in a pool of blood, the blood black as coal in the moonlight.

Shaking with fright, my dad dove under the covers, wide awake now and nearly scared to death himself. He stayed there, shivering underneath the sheets, until his brother unlocked his door the next morning.

In the light of day, no body could be found. But fresh bloodstains covered the floor in my dad's room. The landlord threatened to evict the brothers unless they cleaned up the horrible mess. Despite hours of scrubbing, the two men failed to erase the bloodstains, and were forced to seek lodging elsewhere.

• • •

Sometime later, when my father had established a residence on East 25th Street, he had another odd experience, this one witnessed by many, including, again, his brother.

One day a neighbor lady asked my dad for help.

Each evening about dusk, a ferocious dog would jump onto the woman's porch, snarling and growling.

She feared it was rabid and wanted someone to take care of it. My dad agreed to shoot the dog the next time it came around.

Right on schedule, as the sun was setting the next evening, the dog appeared. Dad, an expert marksman with a pistol, shot the dog from a distance of about 15 feet. Because it was nearly dark, it was difficult to see where the dog had been hit. Though there was no corpse to bury, Dad knew he had at least winged the dog. At the very least, he figured the dog wouldn't come back anytime soon.

A few days later his neighbor called complaining, "I thought you shot that dog," she said. My dad thought he had, too.

It seems that the dog had returned to her porch and had harassed her every night since. Dad shot the dog again, and again the dog disappeared. The next day the dog returned. Dad shot it again. For weeks this routine continued. Although the distance between my dad and the dog varied from night to night, and he couldn't really say for sure that he shot the same animal every time, it looked like the same dog—the same muzzle, the same ears, the same tail, the same snarl.

He tried shooting the dog with a rifle.

All this shooting, not surprisingly, alarmed the neighborhood. After thirty days, someone called the police.

With the police chief on the scene, the ritual played once more. The dog came, was shot, and then disappeared. My father told the chief that this had been happening every night for more than a month. The chief suggested that my dad try a different method, something a little less conventional.

On the chief's advice, Dad went home, melted

down some coins, and made a silver bullet. The next night, he fired that round and the dog was never seen again.

Now it may be pure coincidence, but a lady who lived a block or so away, died that very night. Reportedly, she had no friends and was nasty and argumentative. She had never been known to venture out in the daylight, either.

. . .

Did you get a chuckle out of those tales? The first time I heard them I smiled, too. But my uncle verified every detail, more than twenty years later.

—Journalist, photographer, and heart transplant recipient, Elmer Horton, is a member of the U.S. Coast Guard Auxiliary as well as a charter member of the Department of Homeland Security. He writes a bi-weekly column for the LAKE NORMAN TIMES *and lives in Mooresville, NC.*

2

SOUT

CAT WOMAN'S BRIDGE

CAT WOMAN'S BRIDGE
Chase Gloster

∎

W HERE THE HECK are we, Jim?" asked Suzan.

"We were on South Boulevard, but that just kinda turned into the middle of nowhere." Jim said.

"Well, turn around. I don't wanna get lost out here."

The road twisted like a spring—in this case, a spring wound around a forest, a forest on the outskirts, the outskirts of the city. The road was old, with a streetlight only every mile or so. Here and there an old country house was tucked away from civilization behind the overgrown forest.

"My buddy Jack said this road cuts through to Carmel Road."

"Well, still, I don't like it." Suzan thought her husband should know better than to trust Jack for anything, let alone directions.

"Suzan, we'll be there in no time."

"Whatever—"

They hadn't seen another car for miles. Their radio reception was poor, so the sound of the engine was all they had to listen to. As they approached a bridge at the end of the curve, a streetlight glowed above a yellow BRIDGE FREEZES BEFORE ROAD sign. Over it, someone had tagged "CAT WOMAN'S BRIDGE."

"Hey, I've heard of Cat Woman's Bridge," Suzan said. Tired of the silence, she decided to entertain her husband with a story. "Apparently like, years ago, one of those crazy cat ladies lost one of her cats. She was walking across a bridge near her house looking for it when a car came out of nowhere, slammed right into her, and dragged her across the bridge, killing her. So now she spends eternity searching for her lost cat."

"Hah!" Jim laughed. "You don't believe that stuff do you?"

"Nah, it's just an old story to scare people. Doesn't mean anything to me."

As the two drove across the bridge, Jim looked to his left at the black blanket of woods. THUDTHUD!! THUDTHUD!! The car bounced, violent, yet oddly soft. Jim slammed on the breaks.

"What in the heck was that?" Suzan screamed.

In his rear view mirror Jim could see a lifeless lump sprawled on the street behind them. "Looks like a cat, hon."

She turned to look, "Where?"

"It's right there in the mid—" Jim turned to point at what he'd hit and saw it was no longer there. "Well, it was right there!"

"Oh my gosh, it's probably hurt. Pull over."

Jim pulled off the bridge and parked in the grass. As he stepped out of the car, a slate grey cat dashed beneath the streetlight and disappeared under the bridge. Jim walked slowly back across the bridge, calling for the cat. "Heeere kitty, kitty."

He could hear his voice echo; it sounded strange in the night air, kind of high pitched and strung out. "Heeere kitty, kitty," he continued calling as he climbed down alongside the bridge.

"Heeere kitty, kitty," he heard echoing back to him.

Except it wasn't an echo—it wasn't his voice at all.

A middle-aged woman, barely visible in the pale light from the street lamp, was frantically searching the creek. Her nightgown dragged along the rocks and fallen branches as she waded through the water. "Heeere kitty, kitty."

"Uhh, excuse me?" Jim called to her. "You need some help?"

The woman, crouched low, her face in shadow, said, "I can't see my kitten. Can you see it? Can you see my kitten?"

"Uh, no. I'm afraid I don't know where it is."

The woman continued along the creek bed, shuffling her bare feet in the cold water.

"Um...well, maybe you should come up to the road. My wife and I could help you look there."

"Heeere kitty."

Jim followed the woman, hoping to convince her to return to the road where it was safer. "Eh, excuse me," he said and extended his arm toward her.

She straightened and turned to face Jim full on. Half her face was bloodied; from temple to jaw, asphalt and gravel covered what was left of her skin; one eye was gone, a gaping hole all that was left.

"Oh, my god!" Jim turned and ran up the hill, nearly reaching the top when he felt something grab his leg, pulling him back.

"Heeere kitty."

Jim kicked wildly until finally he broke free. He scrambled up the embankment to the street and did not look back until he reached his car. Out of breath and panicked, he tried to start the engine, but it wouldn't crank.

"Jim what's the matter?" Suzan asked. "What's going on?"

"I don't know! There's some messed up lady down there!" Still the car would not start. Jim peered through the windshield, but it was covered in muddy paw prints.

"Suzan—where did those come from?"

"I don't know."

Finally, the car started. Jim switched on the head-lights, illuminating the disfigured woman who now stood at the hood of the car.

"Have you seen my kitten?" she moaned and hobbled to the passenger window.

Jim floored the accelerator.

Not until the bridge was in the rearview mirror, did the couple breathe a sigh of relief.

Then, the woman, with her cat in her arms, stepped from the woods and into the road. She hobbled directly into their path.

Jim and Suzan screamed.

The moment the car hit her she twisted in agony—it looked as if she'd lived that pain a thousand times over.

And then, she vanished.

Jim and Suzan sat, silent and stunned.

"Jim...?" Suzan said.

"Yea, hon?" he replied and turned to look at her.

She turned to face him. Half her face was bloodied; from temple to jaw, asphalt and gravel covered what was left of her skin; one eye was gone.

"Have you seen my kitten?"

—Born and raised in Charlotte, N.C., Chase Gloster graduated from Myers Park High School and has attended CPCC and UNC-Greensboro. He says he is a "student of twenty years and still getting started!"

3

GRAVITY HILL

GRAVITY HILL

Garrett Brown

■

ON A LONELY stretch of road, between Pfeiffer University and Baden Lake, beyond Mount Pleasant, but before Burlington, there lies possibly the most haunted hill in North Carolina. I dare say even the country.

I don't speak of these things from what I've heard, or from what others have heard through the grapevine.

I have firsthand experience.

Locals call the place Gravity Hill. There's nothing special about the road that it's on. It leads nowhere important, just to another small stretch of road that cuts through a dense spread of trees. Not many cars travel it. There's nothing too special about Gravity Hill— besides its paranormal activity.

Legend has it that soon after the end of World War II, a woman and her baby met their fate on that road. They were rushing to get home, it was getting late, the sun had already set. It seems like cars always break down at the worst times. This happened to be one of them.

The woman's car died. Maybe it was a problem with her engine, maybe she was out of gas, who knows? One thing was certain, after a few minutes of trying to restart the car, her battery was out of juice. She and her baby were stuck that night, smack dab in the middle of nowhere. She'd travelled this way many times and knew the road had a very narrow shoulder. Beyond the pavement there was only a foot, two at the most, of flat ground before a dense thicket took over the landscape. Only at the top of the rise, where a small patch of gravel served to widen the road, would she be safe. With no one there to help her, she knew she'd have to push the vehicle uphill until she reached the summit.

With a dead battery, she had no lights—turn signals, dashboard, headlights—nothing worked. It was so dark now that she could barely see her baby, still sound asleep in the backseat. She put the car in neutral and stepped out into the night air. With her hands centered on the back bumper, she began to push. The car moved slowly at first, but once it gained momentum, it rolled easier uphill, toward the gravel, toward safety.

Before she could reach the top of the hill, a car came barreling up the road. The oncoming driver never saw her. His car slammed into her. The impact flung her car from the road, smashing it into the trees. Mother and baby—both dead.

After that tragic night, folks began to notice that their cars seemed to want to stop along that hill. The engine might hesitate, sometimes stall. Stories sprang up. People swore their cars stopped dead on that road, but then something even stranger would happen.

For a ghostly experience, locals began to say, drive on over to Gravity Hill. That hill became a destination. Over the years, hundreds of kids have left their mark on the fatal spot, their spray painted graffiti stands out like a sore thumb on the lonely stretch of road. The graffiti marks the spot where you stop your car, put it in neutral, sit back and have one of the most frightening experiences of your life.

. . .

My buddies and I decided to give it a try one cold winter night. It was the middle of January and the four of us were bored and ripe for trouble. One of the guys said he knew exactly how to get to Gravity Hill. (Well, not exactly. We got lost a couple times on the curving, country roads.) Somehow we ended up where we needed to be. When the driver of the car pointed to where he'd once spray painted the road, a shiver shot up my spine. I realized that he'd done this before.

He stopped the car on the appropriate spot and popped the gearshift to neutral. We sat there for a second. Nothing happened at first and I thought it was all just a bunch of local superstition.

That was until the car started to roll—*UP* the hill!

All four of us started yelling, but wouldn't dare look behind us. I was certain if I looked out the rear window there'd be a woman, dressed in 1940's garb, pushing our car. She'd be staring at us with a look only a ghost who's doomed to reenact her death every time someone decides to pay her a little visit could have.

Just like the legend goes, our car continued uphill until it reached the spot where the woman and her baby had died those many years before. When it reached that spot, it simply stopped.

If you're a skeptic, then I say try it for yourself. I'm one hundred percent positive any local person will be happy to tell you how to get to Gravity Hill.

Just hope your battery doesn't die.

—Garrett Brown in a native of Concord, N.C. He is a college student, planning to major in English and publish a novel or two.

4

OLD BEN

Old Ben

Robert Troutman Brawley

∎

EVERY MORNING, when the weather was nice, Dr. Augustus Sloop would sit on his front porch, drinking his coffee and reading his Bible.

Every morning, when the weather was nice, he would hear the jingle jangle of harnesses and the creak of wooden wheels, and he would know that Old Ben was on his way to sell his eggs and vegetables to folks in town .

As best as I know, Dr. Sloop moved into his house in the southeast corner of Iredell County around 1847, the exact location where my parents built their house more than a century later in 1965.

Coming from Northern Virginia, where he'd had a very profitable practice, Dr. Sloop chose this area because he thought it would be a good place to raise a family. His slaves, Thomas and Mary, came with him.

Thomas and Mary, a married couple, had been a wedding present when Augustus Sloop wed his bride, Olivia. The Sloops considered Thomas and Mary part of the family and the four soon felt at home in the North Carolina Piedmont.

Sadly, Dr. Sloop lost his wife during childbirth. He named his new daughter Olivia after his wife and put Mary in charge of raising her.

Prior to the War Between the States, Dr. Sloop was known as the best physician between Statesville and Charlotte. As he had done in Virginia, Dr. Sloop built a solid practice here with people coming from miles around for his help. If folks couldn't get to the doc, Thomas would hitch up the buggy and drive the doctor to them. Few people had any real money then, and Dr. Sloop was often paid with chickens, hogs, whiskey or anything else that might be considered of value. Before long, Thomas had a lot of livestock to tend.

During this time, the Sloops' neighbor, Old Ben, farmed and sold his produce to townsfolk. Every morning Old Ben would ride by the Sloops' house and, seeing the doctor on his porch, would holler, "Good morning, doc!" and the doctor would holler back, "Good morning to you, too, Ben!"

When the war began, Dr. Sloop was made a colonel and given command of a large medical corps. He promised Thomas and Mary and his daughter Olivia that he would be gone no more than three months, but it was three years before they saw him again.

In his absence, Thomas and Mary took care of the homeplace and watched over Olivia. The doctor, when he finally returned, seemed to have aged fifty years. The war and its horrors had taken its toll. He stayed in bed for weeks until he got his strength back.

Once he got to feeling better, the doctor decided to sit on his porch with his pipe and Bible and enjoy the sunrise. He heard a sound that he'd almost forgotten. It was Old Ben in his wagon, taking his produce to town. Ben tipped his hat and hollered, "Good morning, doc!" And the doctor hollered back, "Good morning to you, too, Ben!"

The doctor went back to tending the sick—most of his patients were women and children as most of the men had died in battle. He and Ben continued their familiar morning ritual until one day Ben did not come. After a third day without seeing his neighbor, doc got worried. He and Thomas took the buggy down to Ben's farm. The doc called out to Ben but there was no answer.

Dr. Sloop went inside and found Ben dead in his bed. Sad to see his friend gone, the doctor was comforted to know that at least he'd died peacefully.

After the funeral, the doctor continued his morning routine of watching the sunrise and reading his Bible on his front porch. One morning, many months later, the doctor sat outside before dawn and heard the familiar sound of jingling harnesses and wooden wagon wheels. It sounded like Ben's wagon coming up the road. When it got to the doc's house, it stopped. The driver looked at Dr. Sloop and said, "Good morning, doc."

"Is that you, Ben?" the doctor asked, uncertain because the sun was not up yet and it was too dark to see all the way out to the road.

"C'mon and go for a little ride with me."

The doctor climbed into the wagon and saw that it was indeed his neighbor driving the wagon. "Ben, how can you be here?"

"Doc," said Ben, "just relax. We've only got a short way to go."

As they plodded along, it seemed to the doc that it was getting light awful fast. Before they traveled the four miles into town, the sky was the brightest he had ever seen it.

As they rounded the bend, near the flour mill just on the edge of town, the doc saw the biggest crowd he'd ever seen. Hundreds of people were walking behind a flat wagon with a flag-covered casket. Directly behind the wagon was a grand buggy with a finely dressed driver. Ben pulled his wagon to the side and let the crowd pass.

The fancy buggy neared Ben's wagon and doc saw Mary and Thomas and his daughter Olivia inside.

As the crowd walked by, someone said, "What ever will we do without Dr. Sloop?"

The doc looked at Ben, his eyes wide with shock.

Ben smiled and said to his team, "Get along." And off they went.

. . .

On quiet summer mornings I like to sit on my front porch and watch the sun come up over the hill. Sometimes, when the whippoorwills pause from their singing, I think I hear the sounds of an old wagon coming up the road.

I surely hope it doesn't stop just yet.

—Robert Troutman Brawley is a native of Mooresville. After graduating from Lenoir Rhyne College, he returned home to the family seed business. His home, built in 1965 by his grandfather R.W. Troutman, is on the site where Old Ben used to drive his wagon.

5

THE LAKE NORMAN SEA MONSTER
(FIRST SIGHTINGS)

The Lake Norman Sea Monster
(First Sightings)
Larry Douglas Starnes

■

FIVE YOUNG BOYS from Cornelius—my brother and I, another pair of brothers from down the street, and my cousin—all lived on Meridian Street. We ranged in age from eight to twelve when we shared an amazing and unforgettable experience.

This is a true story, as I remember it.

. . .

One Saturday the five of us went camping at a place we called Horseshoe Pit. This place was halfway down our street, across the path that leads to the old Gem Yarn Mill. Forty years ago, this part of town was all wooded. A cleared area, close to the creek, was perfect for camping. Earlier that day, we had gone frog gigging at the pond on Smith Circle, close to Smith's Flower House. With our tote sacks full, we hiked through the woods to our campsite and built a big fire. We'd brought potatoes from home, wrapped in aluminum foil, and we put them in the coals to roast. While the potatoes were cooking, we pitched horseshoes.

Thinking our potatoes should be about ready to eat, I pulled one out of the hot coals. I looked up to tell the others "come and get it" when there—not ten feet from me—stood a black, leathery-looking creature, about five feet tall with a cone-shaped head.

Needless to say, this scared me and I let out a powerful scream. Soon all five of us were screaming and running as fast as we could out of Horseshoe Pit. We were so loud that my mom and dad heard us two blocks away and they came running down Meridian Street to see what was going on. I remember seeing my dad coming toward me and what a welcome sight that was! By the time my parents got to our campsite, the creature was nowhere to be seen.

I was so scared that night I went home and slept in the bed with my parents.

The next day my brother and I, and the rest of our gang, returned to our campsite. We looked carefully to try and find some trace of what we'd seen the night before. We found two footprints that looked kind of human, except they had only three toes. We went home with this new evidence and told everyone about the black, pointy-headed creature that stood about five feet tall and had three toes on each foot. Nobody believed us; everyone just laughed.

About three months later, one of our neighbors, a middle-aged, God-fearing lady, was standing in her kitchen around daybreak. She was washing her frying pan when she saw something coming across the old Gem Yarn Mill path. It came through the field and into her back yard and straight up to her house. It crawled under the porch and began to claw at her floor.

We had party lines in those days, and by the time she got the police on the phone, and they finally arrived, the creature was long gone. When she told everyone what she'd seen, some folks recalled what us kids had reported months before. Our descriptions were identical. People began to talk.

Then, on Highway 115, near McCalls Furniture, in one of the houses near the railroad tracks, another lady caught sight of an odd-looking creature. Out her window, she could see a black, leathery-looking thing with a cone-shaped head staring straight at her. She ran to the bedroom, grabbed a .22 and shot at it—right through her window. Then she called the police. When they arrived they found blood on the railroad tracks. The next day, the police brought dogs to track it. The dogs lost the scent, and that was that.

. . .

For the next seven years, I heard tales of people who'd seen the same kind of creature. There were sightings off and on along the eastern side of Lake Norman.

Back then, Lake Norman was only a few years old, with very few houses on it. A friend of mine and his date parked one night out on Highway 73 at Ramsey Creek, just an overgrown cove at the time. All of the sudden, something black, with a pointed head, came out of the water and hit the trunk of the car with two fists. My friend cranked his engine and sped away. I surely did see the dents in his car. I heard other teenagers' blood-curdling tales about what they saw at "Spook Gully" which was on the lake near the dam. One man claimed he was chased back to shore while fishing in the "Little Lake" (Lake Cornelius) by some black and leathery thing.

Last time I heard about the creature I was sixteen. Heard it on the radio. Apparently, the creature had wandered into some lady's yard around Statesville. According to the radio, the thing would come out of the woods late in the evening, and just stand and stare at her. Her dog would bark at it, then run under the house and hide. The radio station organized a "Lake Norman Sea Monster Hunt," scheduled for that Saturday, but it was later cancelled due to rain.

Nowadays, the only time I hear of the monster is if my brother or cousin bring it up. We just shake our heads and laugh, but we all know what we saw and we'll never forget.

Even now, I can close my eyes and still see that black, cone-headed monster. Even now, when I am out at night, or in the woods, I find myself looking over my shoulder. An eerie feeling comes over me.

Some say, there's nothing out there at night that's not there at day.

I think otherwise. Some things *only* come out at night.

—*Larry Starnes grew up in Cornelius, N.C. After graduating from North Mecklenburg High School, he served as a sniper during the Vietnam War. He and his wife Paula, his high school sweetheart, have two daughters and five grandchildren.*

6

THE CURSE OF OLIPHANT'S MILL

The Curse of Oliphant's Mill

Shaughn Tohill

■

MANY YEARS AGO, along the banks of a creek that fed the mighty Catawba River, John Oliphant, a settler from Pennsylvania, built a gristmill. The creek became known as Oliphant's Creek and the town that sprang up around the gristmill became known as Oliphant's Mill.

The Thomasons, Whites, and the Lawsons farmed there, growing cotton with the help of their fieldhands and slaves. Decades passed and the Civil War ravaged towns throughout the South, including Oliphant's Mill. Many families ceased farming after the war and moved to Charlotte. Now free, the former slaves began anew—sometimes living in the homes of their former owners, trying to make what was once hell, home.

Not much changed until the early 1950s when a plan for damming the Catawba River to create another "power lake" began to surface. Men in suits—seldom a good sign in the country—began visiting the slaves' descendants, informing them of their homes' impending demolition. Most residents left willingly due to the monetary consideration and promises of shoreline real estate on the future Lake Norman, but some quailed at the thought of desecrating the graves of their ancestors. Burying them a second time, this time in water, didn't sit well.

One way or another, Duke Power Company convinced everyone to leave, and the Lake Norman groundbreaking was held September, 1959. It took four years to build the dam and another two years to fill the lake. At last, Duke Power had its lake, but they also had something else—a curse.

One of the last to leave Oliphant's Mill, Annabelle Cooke had learned occult arts from her mother, as her mother had from her mother, as it had been for generations. Annabelle's 16-year-old son had drowned in the Catawba River many decades before. After drinking moonshine with his buddies, he was lost to the river's swift currents. Days later his body surfaced and Annabelle wept over the bloated, nearly unrecognizable remains of her only son. Now, in her old age, Annabelle's thoughts still dwelt on her lost son and the thought of his grave being covered in water, forever haunting him with the very cause of his death, stirred an anger deep within her.

The curse was simple: a few bones, some blood, and whispered names set the anathema in place.

Lake Norman did not really become a destination until the completion of I-77. Even then, it was many years before people began vacationing and building homes there. Annabelle's curse rested just under the surface, unnoticed and waiting.

A young couple visiting family in Davidson were its first victims.

Eyewitnesses to the boating mishap described what looked like a flag sticking straight out of the water. The flag was attached to a boat, a boat which had sunk, but was being held at the surface by a large air pocket in the fore of the vessel. Divers found the bodies some 20 yards away at the bottom of the lake. It appeared that the couple had drowned without life vests, two miles from shore. The accident report said that numerous leaks were discovered in the boat, and that the man's blood alcohol level was 1.6, the woman's 1.0.

Two more accidents occurred soon after, both at night, both involving alcohol, and both caused by numerous leaks in the boat. The first took four lives; the second claimed one lone soul.

A few months ago, a woman rented a pontoon boat to entertain five of her sorority sisters. She knew a cool spot near her condo that had a great view of the million dollar homes that line the shores of Lake Norman. The area was also secluded enough to have a good time without worrying about lake patrol interference.

Around ten o'clock that night, the girls were getting a little tipsy when their hostess noticed the boat was tipping. She thought she'd drunk too much wine, but when she felt the boat shift more, she knew something was wrong.

She walked to the steering wheel to get her bearings. The horizon line was slowly and steadily rising— parallel to the woman's panic.

"The boat is sinking!" she screamed.

Conversation stopped.

"Grab a life vest!" She put one on and began tossing others toward her friends.

Somewhat sobered by their hostess' alarm, the girls now recognized the danger. At the same time, the front of the boat dipped below the surface of the lake. Then they heard a faint chant.

> *"He died in water,*
> *so shall you*
> *if you drink*
> *the devil's brew."*

This is what the tear-stained woman told police after she was found floating about a half-mile from where her boat had sunk. Unfortunately, none of her friends had survived. Inebriated and therefore unable to maneuver life vests, the five had all drowned.

The police told her that moving water makes many different sounds. They said that she'd probably mistook the sound of the rushing water for a whisper. But she knew. She had heard the words clearly, as if dictated directly to her. She also knew she was lucky to be alive.

When she told me her story, I recalled the other stories I'd heard. Like the others, hers involved alcohol. I asked the woman to tell me the location of the cove where she'd anchored her boat.

And then it was clear.

That cove had once been a tributary of the mighty Catawba—a creek. A creek where John Oliphant, a settler from Pennsylvania, had once built a gristmill. The gristmill that had become the town of Oliphant's Mill. The town where Annabelle Cooke's son was buried.

Before you set sail on Lake Norman at night,

before you pop open a beer, or uncork a bottle of wine, remember Oliphant's Mill and Annabelle Cooke.

—College student and bartender, Shaughn Tohill, claims he is one of the last "born and raised Charlotte natives around." He lives with his roommate Lyndsey and their two dogs, Carmen and Althea.

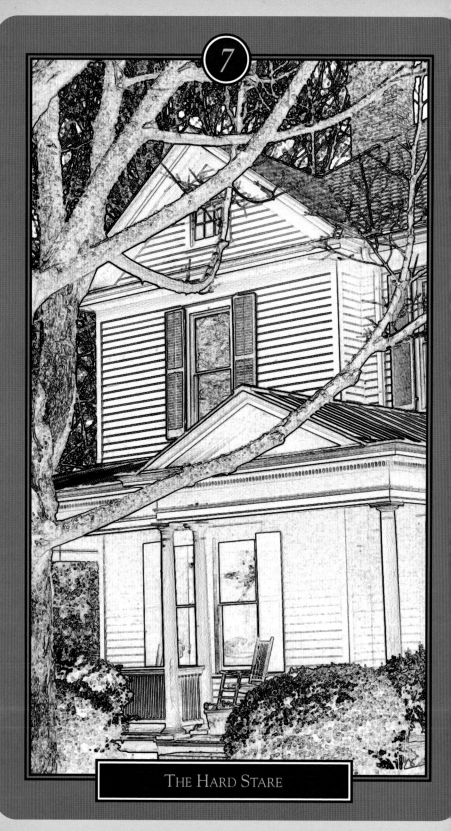

7

THE HARD STARE

The Hard Stare

Gill Holland

■

MISS OLIVE LASHBACK lived to be a hundred, there in her Victorian house on Davidson's Concord Road. Miss Olive was healthy and long-lived; her father had been born when George Washington was still alive.

My friends and I enjoyed many a pleasant visit with the woman in our youth for she could tell a good tale. Her voice was clear and mellow, her face animated. If she asked us questions though, we had to write our responses on a piece of paper, for she was stone deaf.

One day she told us a story about her father. "He was a nervous man, a very nervous man, but he was a gentleman—an Old Testament gentleman." He had been fond of quoting scripture, especially passages like: "The fear of the Lord is the beginning of wisdom." "For whom the Lord loveth he correcteth; even as a father the son in whom he delighteth." "Thou shalt beat thy son with the rod, and shalt deliver his soul from hell."

"My father was the only surviving son," she said. "His brothers all died in infancy which was not unusual back in that day. He married my mother late in life; I myself was born at the end of the Civil War. While my father loved us all, he did beat my brothers," Miss Olive reminisced. "Never his daughters, though.

"As a little boy my father experienced a ghastly mal-adventure with President Washington, or I should say, Washington's spectral self.

"Washington died in 1799, when my father was five years old. One December day the president rode for hours in the snow. He returned to Mount Vernon, but the beastly quinsy attacked him and the doctors finished him off with bleedings and a blister of cantharides."

I scrawled "cantharides" across my paper, and added a large question mark.

"My father loved that word," she said squinting at my paper. "He told me cantharides was just a fancy word for ground-up beetles."

My friends and I looked at each other. No wonder he died.

Miss Olive continued with her tale. "Everybody in the country knew President Washington's last words," and then she quoted them to us:

I die hard, but I am not afraid to go... Let me go off quietly. I cannot last long.

"'I die hard.'" Miss Olive repeated the phrase again, "'I die hard.' Those words lingered in the minds of many and those same words will give you a hint of what came to haunt my poor father.

"Years before, when General Washington became President, there was a statue erected in the town square. It was a wooden statue, all painted white, placed high on a pedestal. Washington's face stared hard, looking down at all who passed. When word of his death reached town, people speculated that President Washington left this world with that same hard stared fixed on his face—unafraid and ready to meet his Maker.

"One night, just before Christmas and soon after Washington's death, my father was in bed. He remembered he had a stomachache because of the excitement of the Season. His dog Snowball was under the covers with him. It had snowed all day, but was clear and cold that night. A half moon rose in the sky. Suddenly, he heard something in the corner of his room. He looked toward the window and saw a shimmering form, as white as the snow outside. The figure just stood there, looking out the window with a hard stare.

"Snowball crawled out from under the bedclothes. When the dog saw the figure he gave a yelp. Father ducked his head under the covers and squeezed his eyes closed. He prayed aloud, 'Help us, Jesus, oh help us!'

"Awhile later, when he dared to peek, the white specter had vanished. The boy and his dog trembled, but eventually went back to sleep. The next morning, my father told his parents what had happened. His father answered, 'Well, son, I hope you learned something from General Washington's visit.'

"'Oh, Mr. Lashback,' (my grandmother called her husband that) 'how can you say that? General Washington, indeed! The boy was terrified.'

"'Is the Lord's hand waxed short?' (My grandfather loved to quote Numbers 11:23. He could make it mean anything.)

"The spectre appeared night after night. Soon, my father became afraid to go upstairs. He would cry as his father carried him to bed. His mother wept, too.

"The little dog Snowball seemed to go crazy and finally ran away."

Miss Olive sighed. "I don't think my father ever got over the grim general's nightly visitations. The spectre haunted him well into adulthood. My mother told me he would attend séances and ask the medium to conjure General Washington. Once, he even had a daguerreotype made of the visitant spirit. I saw the picture once when I was little. It was white like a ghost. It haunted me, too, for a while.

"Not until his father died, did his mother reveal the secret." Miss Olive looked at us. "Can you guess what it was?"

Awestruck, we could not think of a thing to write on our papers.

"What is the most horrible thing the secret could have been?" She coaxed us to imagine what it could be.

We could only shake our heads.

"The ghastly white spectre was his father, my grandfather. He wanted his child to learn fear. And he did. That fear has passed down the generations. We watch everyone in the family to see if they show signs of mental problems. So far, no one has."

That was our last visit with Miss Olive for a spell.

—The Holland family has lived just outside Davidson for years. Gill teaches English at Davidson College. He and his wife, Siri, remember a party in Miss Lashback's house in the early 1960s.

SOME HELP FROM UNCLE ED

SOME HELP FROM UNCLE ED

Larry Paul

■

I AM A HOUSE PAINTER of Native American descent. Often, I can sense the energy and presence of old souls while I'm working, but I'd never had concrete evidence of such until I painted Uncle Ed's house.

My friend's uncle had lived in the same house for well over 40 years. The house, built in the 1920s, had textured plaster walls and ceilings. My friend explained that Ed, a widower with no children of his own, had passed away in his bedroom a few months before, and had left his nephew (my friend) in charge of the estate. He warned me that the house, which was some distance away from Charlotte, was not in good shape. He'd tried to hire a local contractor to make repairs, but things had not progressed smoothly. He hired me and my co-worker Tony to repaint the interior of the house.

My friend and his son were going to spend the

weekend working on the second floor plumbing. Tony and I planned to arrive a day ahead of them and prep the entire house for painting.

When Tony and I arrived Friday, we unlocked the door and walked inside. My friend had not exaggerated. Major repairs were in order, nearly a third of the ceiling had water damage. Water damage extended along the walls in many rooms. It looked—and felt—as if the house had been weeping. I immediately felt a presence there. It was guarded—a curious, but alert sensation.

What are you doing in my house?

Tony and I unloaded the truck and carried the paint sprayer and other equipment inside. The mood in the house took on a more passive feel.

Oh, you're here to do some work.

We spent the night at a nearby motel.

. . .

The next morning, on the way to Uncle Ed's house, Tony mentioned that he'd felt something in the house the night before. He asked if I'd felt anything. I admitted that I had.

We decided to start in a room that needed only wall repairs. Now, I have worked on a variety of textured surfaces and have been able to match most with no trouble. Here, I couldn't quite figure out the correct tool or technique to get it to blend just right.

Later, my friend and his son arrived and suggested that I poke around in the basement. Uncle Ed had an area devoted to old paint, tools and supplies. I searched, but to no avail.

Without the right brush, we couldn't go any

further on the walls. We decided to tackle some of the major ceiling repair work instead. After several coats of quick drying plaster as a base, it was time to clean my tools. I went to use an old wash tub sink in the basement.

The basement was filled with stacks of boxes and paper bags that still had to be sorted by the family. Being a house painter, I know trust is important in this business. I never snoop through people's belongings—living or deceased. But, in order to get to the sink I had to pass all these bags and boxes, so I did casually glance to see if a texture brush was visible. Nothing there.

After cleaning my tools, I started back towards the basement stairs. I had an overwhelming sensation to stop. I literally could not take one more step. I stood there for a moment and looked at the bags near me. One bag in particular seemed to draw me closer.

Look here.

With much hesitation, I moved a couple of pieces of loose paper with the tip of my finger. There, under some old envelopes, sat a texture brush.

I ran upstairs to tell Tony that Uncle Ed had found us the exact brush we needed. My friend's son heard me say something about Uncle Ed and came downstairs. His dad followed.

I related the story of my discovery and then my friend told me he had had a similar experience in the basement.

After several days, Tony and I both could feel that Uncle Ed was happy with the work we were doing. My only regret was that we couldn't have made these changes to the house while he was still living. We sensed, though, that he was content and pleased to know that our work would help in the sale of the home, which in turn would benefit the remaining members of his family.

Thanks for the help Uncle Ed, couldn't have done it without you.

—Larry has a degree in Writing Arts from the State University of NY, Oswego. He was a photojournalist in the army and has lived in the Charlotte area for more than 16 years. Currently he is a painting contractor who is getting back into writing and photography.

9

MORE HELP FROM UNCLE ED

More Help from Uncle Ed
Peterson

■

a FEW WEEKS AGO I dined at a restaurant that prepared steaks the traditional ways: rare, medium, and well done, but also offered another: Chicago-style— charred and crispy on the outside and any way you like on the inside. I immediately thought of my late Uncle Ed, a Chicago-style kind of guy if ever there was one.

Uncle Ed was known for wanting things *his* way, and firmly believing that his way was not just the *best* way, but the *only* way. With him there was no negotiating, no compromise. Childless, Ed had maintained a close relationship with his nephews; my three brothers and I were like sons to him. Always he had advice for us—advice he liked to dispense over dinner. Dinner with Ed was an event, one that was often embarrassing for his dinner companions, neighboring tables, and wait staff.

"I want a steak and I want it WELL DONE." He'd

fix a stare on the waiter and give him further instructions, "Tell your chef back there that I don't want to see
even a hint of pink. Don't butterfly it, either. If it's a bit
crunchy around the edges, now that's okay with me."

Ed's steak would arrive and invariably be returned
to the kitchen. "How is it that I can make a steak at
home perfectly," he would say to the waiter, steak knife
in hand, "but you, with your fancy equipment and
supposedly well-trained chef, can't?" He'd jab at the
(what to him was an obviously undercooked) piece of
meat and say, "Send it back." Many times, Ed would
summon the chef to his table and ask him face to face
why he couldn't properly cook a steak.

Dining quietly was rarely an option with Ed.

Widowed ten years earlier, Ed died in August 2005,
at home and alone. As executor of his will, I had an
ominous responsibility because, as with all things, Ed
wanted his estate handled *his* way. Years before he told
me that I'd find a red binder with explicit instructions. I
was to follow these instructions to the letter.

At the time of his death, Ed's house was in poor
condition. Due to an accident that had crippled his right
hand, he had been unable to keep up with basic mainte-
nance, but too proud to ask for help. Water had
damaged the ceilings, age and neglect left the plaster
walls cracked. The carpets had worn away, revealing the
hardwood floors underneath. And, like so many people
who had lived through the Depression, Ed believed that
if something still worked, or had the slightest possibility
of being repaired, it should be saved. Consequently, Ed
had amassed quite a collection of things—some of value,
some not. My brothers and I found suitcases, packed
with long outdated vacation attire, stacks of newspapers,

grocery bags, books of trading stamps, bicycle parts, old alarm clocks, can openers, keyrings, flashlights, door-knobs, and what looked to be receipts for every purchase Ed ever made. Ed saved envelopes, too, and used them as scratch paper. It was eerie finding little notes that he'd left for himself.

Buy eggs, milk. Call Mary Tuesday.

Wading through all the clutter, I realized that the first thing we had to do was rent a dumpster.

Much to the dismay of the neighbors, a dumpster was plunked down in Ed's front yard. I promised them we'd have the dumpster gone in two days. My brothers and I wasted no time, making short work of tossing Ed's old stuff. However, when silver certificates fluttered from between the pages of an outdated coin collector catalog, our pace slowed considerably.

We began discovering gems hidden amongst the junk. The cleanup effort took on the atmosphere of a treasure hunt. We found an extensive coin collection (half of which was under the dining room table), uniforms from Ed's stint in the Korean War, and my aunt's jewelry. I also found letters and cards that my children had sent him over the years. We found dolls that he'd purchased, presumably as Christmas presents for his great-nieces.

My youngest brother dove into the dumpster and pulled a lot of stuff back out, unwilling to take the chance that we'd mistakenly tossed something valuable.

We spent two days sorting. We gave a lot to the neighbors, filled the garage with items that could be donated to charity; things we wanted to keep we stored in the living room. The four of us worked well into the night of the second day, the night before Ed's funeral.

Satisfied that we'd salvaged everything of value, we called it a day. All we had left was a pile of trash in the basement waiting to go into the dumpster. I told my brothers that I'd stop by the house first thing the next morning to take out the last of the trash. I had already arranged for the dumpster to be hauled away the next morning.

As I unlocked the door the next morning, I heard an alarm. I followed the sound to the basement where, on a table piled three feet high with bags of trash destined for the dumpster, an old smoke alarm was working overtime. Removing its battery, I wondered how many years this smoke detector had been lying around the basement. I wondered why it had chosen this particular morning to start sounding its alarm.

"Ed," I said, "are you here?"

Immediately, the fluorescent light above the table began blinking on and off. There was no one else in the house and even if there were a prankster, a fluorescent light does not turn on and off like that—like an incandescent bulb controlled by a switch.

I had a strong feeling that I should take a closer look at the table. On top of the table sat a black Hefty bag full of old papers and used envelopes.

I said, "Ed, is there something I need to know?"

The light continued to flash on, off, on, off.

I opened the trash bag and saw an old FedEx envelope. When I lifted the envelope I could feel that there was definitely something in it. Indeed there was— $100,000 worth of U.S. savings bonds to be exact.

"Ed," I said, "Don't worry. I found the savings bonds." I held them in the air. "I've got them."

Immediately, the light stopped flashing and the basement went dark.

Later that day, my brothers and I and our families met at the funeral home. The viewing room was outfitted exactly as Ed had specified. We'd found a few photos of Ed and his wife Gerry, and we tucked in with the flowers, the only deviation we made to Ed's carefully scripted directions. My oldest brother Roland thanked the funeral director for preparing the room so nicely. When he commented that he thought Ed would be pleased, a lamp near Ed's casket began flashing. The funeral director said he would have someone check the bulb right away. Roland told him not to bother. "There's nothing wrong with the bulb. It's Ed. He's letting us know that he's pleased with the preparations."

Then the bulb stopped flashing.

Like his steaks, Ed was a tough individual—on the outside. He lived in a crusty old house, and had a lot of crusty old stuff, but buried in his belongings we found some sweet treasures. Underneath Ed's tough exterior was a sweet gentle man who made sure that his nephews were well taken care of after his death.

It's taken two years to liquidate Ed's estate. I cannot believe it was pure chance that I happened upon a restaurant that made a steak exactly as Ed would have liked it just as I'm completing my duties his executor. The Chicago-style steak was more than that. It was another communication from Ed, his way of letting me know all is well.

—Peterson lives in North Carolina with his dog and a cat, his three beautiful children, and wife of 23 years. It keeps getting better.

10

ME & LEE

ME & LEE
WILSON CREEK ADVENTURES

Jeff L. Shook

■

MY BROTHER Lee and I used to hike up Schoolhouse Ridge and camp. Like a lot of teenagers in those days, setting up camp for us included breaking out some whiskey. We'd have a couple drinks and sit around playing cards and shooting the breeze. Nights when the moon wasn't out, Schoolhouse Ridge would be as black as a cave; the stars looked like glitter flung across the sky.

In the stillness of the pitch black night, we could hear just about everything—even the slightest little sound. We could tell critters were out there scuttling around and such. There used to be an old dog nobody could get close to that wandered through the woods. It had a very unusual bark. We'd hear and see it during the day as we went up the ridge. Though we never really heard anything from him as evening came on, we'd wonder if he was out there watching us.

One night we heard something in the distance, down the ridge from our campsite. The sound of crunching leaves signalled someone's—or something's—approach, but we couldn't see a thing. Gradually, odd lights appeared, glimmering through the thicket—a kind of light unlike any light produced by man-made devices.

We could make out three distinct lights moving toward our campsite. The sound of someone—or something—moving over fallen leaves grew louder. Lee and I were scared to death but it was so dark we were afraid to move away from the campfire. We picked up sticks, rocks, anything within sight and began throwing them in the direction of the lights. The lights continued toward us until they got within twenty to thirty yards of our campsite. We were completely panicked by now.

But, within another half a minute or so, the lights vanished.

We kept a close watch the rest of the night. The next day, we searched the area where the lights had appeared, but all we found were the sticks and rocks we'd thrown.

This experience stayed with me a long while. I spent a lot of time reading all the scientific explanations of those mysterious lights that I could get my hands on. None of them seemed plausible, not considering what my brother and I had seen up close. Locals told me the lights had been around for years; they called them the Brown Mountain Lights. Folklore suggests that the lights are really Cherokee squaws looking for their husbands who were lost in battle. I still wondered what they *really* were.

. . .

My brother was a bit more fearless and stuff like mysterious lights didn't bother him for long. Lee's fearless nature got us into some crazy situations. Most people would just think of crazy stuff to do; we DID it!

An old abandoned hotel that everyone called the Dodge House, stood next to the Edgemont Baptist Church cemetery. The two of us had been to the hotel many times during the day and knew the place like the backs of our hands. Once, when a bunch of friends and a couple cousins were visiting, we got to partying and my brother got the big idea to take everyone to the Dodge House Hotel. My brother figured we'd scare the living heck out of them. My pit bull Pirate, with his spiked collar and stocky build, looked intimidating, so we took him along for added security.

We found an old broom with the bristles all but gone and soaked it in kerosene. Once we lit a match to it, we had a great torch to light our way. Just inside the front door, an old piano was still there, along with the check-in counter and some couches. I lagged behind for a moment to play a couple of spooky chords on the piano as my brother led the others up the staircase. The broom torch, burning strong, illuminated the tour.

We went from room to room, spooking the others as we opened doors. Part of the hotel had fallen away, leaving a second story drop-off in one room. Beyond the door, all that was left was some exposed plumbing and a toilet which was suspended in midair. Lee and I had figured this would be the scariest part of the night.

We were wrong.

Smoke started to billow off the broom and the light flickered when we opened the next door. There, in the middle of the room, we saw a rolled up rug with two boots sticking out one end. Lee and I exchanged a look that said, *Where did this come from?* At that moment the broom torch expired, casting only an eerie reddish-orange glow that barely lit our faces, let alone what might have been lurking around us.

The floors began to creak from footsteps that couldn't be ours because all of us were standing frozen in place—more scared than we'd ever been. Poor Pirate was so frightened that he seemed glued to my side. Panic struck and we took off, scrambling down the stairs, wanting nothing more than to reach the door.

We leaped over the last four or five steps and jumped off the hotel porch. In shock, we laughed, glad to have escaped with our lives.

. . .

Lee passed away in a freak tractor accident a couple years ago. I miss his sense of adventure. Without him along, I'm too scared to do things like we used to. After his funeral, the family gathered at home. We were outside, reminiscing about old times, when our pit bull Rascal (Pirate had gone on to his great reward sometime after the Great Hotel Caper), started barking. Like Pirate before him, this dog wasn't scared of much. He headed up the driveway, toward the hollar where Lee's accident had occurred. My sisters followed the dog.

As they neared the road, they saw a weird, reddish light. It was glowing faintly and moving slowly through the hollar. Rascal turned, tucked his tail, and ran back down the driveway as if something was after him. My sisters felt a slight breeze and could smell my brother's cologne. It put goose bumps on them—they couldn't believe what was happening. It didn't really scare them; they thought it was Lee's way of letting them know he was still here with them.

Later that evening, a bunch of us played darts like Lee and his friends had for years. I was playing a game and was dominating the score, just like Lee used to do. I needed three bullseye throws to close out the game and said, "Lee, if you can hear me, help me make these shots." Well, I made those shots, and won by a big margin. As I made my last throw, one of my cousins photographed me in motion. The print shows a glowing, streaming sweep of color right next to me.

Lee's funeral was at Edgemont Baptist Church, an absolutely beautiful church about a century old. He rests in the cemetery beside the church, which is next to what used to be the old Dodge House Hotel. One day I took a picture of the church. In the print an unusual reddish swoop sweeps above the church. When I show it to people, a lot of folks say, "Aaww that's just an imperfection in the print."

If you saw it, and knew what we knew, you'd know it was Lee.

—Jeff Shook was born in Charlotte, N.C. In the 1970s, his parents acquired a vacation home in Wilson Creek, part of the wild and scenic Brown Mountain Gorge. He earned a marketing degree from ECU and has since purchased and renovated the Brown Mountain Lodge, complete with a 12-foot water wheel.

11

MOUNTAIN WANDERER

MOUNTAIN WANDERER
LADY OF THE MOUNTAINS

Joyce Marie Sheldon

■

A S A CHILD, Carolina spent her days hiking through the Smoky Mountains. "Carolina, Carolina," the mountains whispered, like someone with a secret meant just for her. She'd wander over the rocky terrain, searching for the source of the voice that only she could hear. When she grew tired, she would sit, basking in the sun, feeling as if the mountains' welcoming arms surrounded her.

Carolina grew to love the mountains. Nothing— and no one—could come close to the beauty, the rapture, the mystery of their gentle grace and awe inspiring wonder. Each day, as Carolina awoke, she greeted the mountains aloud as if they were a companion in the same room. "Good morning, my beautiful mountains," she would say as she parted her bedroom curtains.

"Carolina, Carolina," the mountains would

whisper, like someone with a secret meant just for her.

"I love you," she would whisper back.

Carolina became a poet whose work reflected her love of the mountains and their mystery. Her fame grew and even at the height of her success, her needs remained simple, her desires singular—nothing held meaning or value beyond her mountains. They stood at her shoulder as she wrote. They listened when she needed a friend. The comfort and consolation they provided attracted her like an irresistible, magnetic force. The echo of their spirit became her very breath.

"Carolina, Carolina," the mountains whispered, like someone with a secret meant just for her.

Carolina followed the voice of the mountains, hiking their trails in every type of weather, conversing with them as if they were human. At best, the towns-people thought her eccentric. They called her the Mountain Wanderer, The Lady of the Mountains. Stories of her odd behavior circulated through the town and wound down the mountainside. Carolina did not know, nor did she care, what people said about her. Her pleasure was found in the mountains, and as long as she could hear them calling her name, she was content.

In her later years, the quiet time of her life as she called it, Carolina went to bed each night in the glow of the mountains' purple shadows. Every morning, Carolina awoke to the whisper of her name which swirled around their smoky peaks. "Carolina, Carolina," the mountains whispered, like someone with a secret meant just for her. She stirred to the gentle awakening, her beloved mountains, the first thing she saw each day.

One autumn morning, she awoke to see her moun-tains hidden in fog. When she sat at her desk to write, the words did not filter onto the page. Carolina could not hear herself think.

She watched the fog as it rose, wafting ever upward, then disappearing like a magician's trick.

Still, no words came to her. The page in front of Carolina remained blank. Surely the mountains would inspire her, she thought. Surely. Carolina tucked some bread and cheese in her pockets, pulled on a pair of old hiking boots and headed out with her notebook and pen in hand.

Carolina walked a trail near her home. A vibrant mantle of red and gold tipped the leaves of summer.

"Carolina, Carolina," the mountains whispered, like someone with a secret meant just for her.

She continued up the mountain, stopping here and there along the way to soak in the beauty of the day. The path became difficult and Carolina stumbled. Her breathing became labored.

In a small clearing, on a patch of weathered grass, brown now that summer was dying, she sat and opened her notebook. The words came—

> *Whispering winds gently*
> *blow the days and years.*
> *Evening tides sweep away*
> *fear and doubt.*
>
> *Shadowed glow of purple*
> *moonlight warms my fragile spirit.*
> *Roaring waves of early dawn*
> *renew my weary soul.*

"Carolina, Carolina," the mountains whispered,

like someone with a secret meant just for her.

"I hear you," she said.

They found her weeks later, curled around her last lines of poetry, resting on a pillow of autumn leaves, her body almost perfectly preserved by the heavenly air of the mountains she loved so dearly.

• • •

In October, when the chill of the season seeps into the valleys, townspeople resurrect the tales of the Mountain Wanderer, the Lady of the Mountains, who so loved the purple mountains that she lay down and died with them. They say Carolina still wanders through the hills of the Smoky Mountains—following the voice that echoed in her heart all the days of her life—the voice to which she finally responded in utter completeness.

—Joyce Marie Sheldon is the author of "From Fear to Faith, A Caregiver's Journey." Based on her personal experiences with The Power of Acceptance, she shares her insight and embraces her mission of inspiring and nurturing the spiritual well-being of others, especially those in the role of caregiver. Her second book, "Seekers and Dreamers," will be published late 2007.

12

FALL

Fall

Kristen J. Fortin

∎

OUTSIDE MY WINDOW I see a cluster of red leaves dance in circles around the mailbox. Next to me, Rags wags his tail. He focuses on the door, hoping I will open it and take him for a walk.

"Not today, Raggedy," I say as I touch the cold glass of the window.

Rags persists, adding an excited whimper and a half jump toward the door. He's an energetic Springer Spaniel and I know that if I don't take him out he will be climbing all over the couch like a crazed mountain goat. One of his long curly ears has flopped inside out and he quivers with excitement as I get his leash from the hook near the garage.

"Okay, Rags, you win," I tell him and I take my jacket from the hall closet. I clip the leash to Rag's frayed collar and open the door. He bolts and pulls hard on the leash, hopping like a rabbit against my resistance.

We walk to the end of our street and turn toward Harris Road Middle School to check on the bridge reconstruction. Harris Road has been blocked for several months and I am curious to see what has been going on behind the detour signs.

We pass the ROAD CLOSED sign and look at the construction of the new school; red clay shines in the cold October air. The bend in the road yields a new view of the old bridge. No longer is it a two-lane crossing with yellow hourglass warning signs posted on both sides. Now it is four lanes, with orange stripes and reflective disks down the center. No one is around and the bridge looks finished so I take a tentative first step onto the virgin asphalt. Rags stops tugging at the leash and I have to drag him behind me. I inch along the bridge. Halfway across I hear a loud "whoosh, whoosh." Rags tangles the leash around my ankles and cowers between my feet.

My heart races. I peek over the edge of the bridge. Rocky River is a thin stream of water twisting through countless catfish skeletons. The sight of bones startles me. Suddenly five vultures, with wings wider than I am tall, fly out from under the bridge—just inches below the soles of my shoes. The rush of wind from their wings hits my face. I see one drop something from its talons. The object makes a dull clank as it hits the bridge. I run toward it. It's an old skeleton key. I put the key in my pocket and suddenly the world is still and silent.

The birds fly into the woods beyond the bridge. There, between two gum trees, I catch a glimpse of corrugated tin. It is the roof of a dilapidated, two-story house I have never before seen. A single shutter clings to one of three broken windows. A tangle of vegetation has overtaken the yard. Rags breaks free from the leash and dashes towards the house.

"No, Rags!" I sprint after him. He vanishes in the tall grass and reappears inside the house, sitting at the window. Thoughts dart through my mind so quickly that I cannot capture them. Each step towards the house seems to take me further from it. I stop to catch my breath, and look up to see the old house is now just a few feet in front of me. I know it was not that close a moment ago. Chills run up my spine. One of the vultures perches on the porch roof and picks apart a snake. There is no sign of Rags. I feel I am being watched. There is no one here. Just get Rags and go. I see no one but I hear the sing-song chanting of a child.

"Raggedy, Raggedy, Raggedy-Roo. Where did you go? What did you do?"

The chanting repeats.

"Raggedy, Raggedy, Raggedy-Roo. Where did you go? What did you do?"

I am breathless, both from running and terror. I creep onto the porch. The vulture remains. I try the doorknob; it's locked. The key, I remember. I fumble with it. The knob turns. Without taking a step I am drawn into the house. Another second passes, and in a blur I am standing on the second-story window sill. I see Rags by the road, sitting at the bridge. A vulture squats on the floor behind me and regurgitates an eyeball of a dead possum. I smell mildew and carrion.

The voice sings again.

"Hop your scotch and jump if you dare. I once fell when I was there."

And then I feel a push on my shoulders. For what seems like a full minute I watch as the jagged rocks on the ground below race towards me. I land on a tuffet of soft grass.

"*One was pushed and one was caught. Life leaves some that death forgot. Tit for tat makes this a draw. Forget what's here and all you saw.*"

In an instant, I am home, standing at my window, watching red leaves dance in circles around the mailbox. Rags stands next to me, hoping for a walk. I run to the closet and fling open the door. I thrust my shaking hand into the pocket of my jacket. I feel the rusty surface of a skeleton key. I jump as my husband comes in through the garage. I make him drive me to the construction site. I won't tell him why.

There is no bridge—only bulldozers and cranes and red clay shining in the cold October air.

—Originally from Ventura County, California, Kristen Fortin received a B.A. from the University of California, Berkeley. Before moving to North Carolina in 2004, she worked as a Ventura County police officer. Her first book, "Lala Strong and Brave," was published in 2007. She now lives in Concord, N.C. with her husband and their son Davis.

13

JACK-O'-LANTERNS

JACK-O'-LANTERNS

Sandra H. Yokely

■

IN A CORNER of Davidson County, near the Forsyth County line, lies an ancient burial ground. Native American tribes laid their dead to rest here. Now, it is overgrown with poplar and pine. No stone markers, just the whisper of souls, the scent of sulphur.

Anyone brave enough to venture into these woods in the clear light of day will probably find a few arrow heads. But they will also notice an eerie feeling of danger hanging in the air above the trampled ground. A strange, lingering scent of grease and smoke will tease their nostrils.

At night when the sky is black and moonless, these woods come alive. In the dark of the night, strange lights appear. As the night grows darker, the lights grow brighter. The wind adds its lonely chant. As the wind whistles through the trees, the lights weave up and down in their dance of death. The dance grows more intense and the lights intensify. Soon the woods are full of these mysterious lights. Locals, some of them descended from the tribes that prospered there long ago, say this is the signal that their warrior ancestors are preparing for battle.

A man called Victor laughed at the locals when he heard them talk about the mysterious flickering lights in the forest. Convinced that the lights were nothing more than jack-o'-lanterns lit with candles, he decided to go into the woods one night and see for himself.

Before Victor ventured very far into the forest, his nostrils were filled with an eerie odor. Ghostly figures danced around him, drawing him deeper into the woods.

At the center of the forest, in a clearing of trampled grass, ghostly fingers grabbed at Victor, leaving him powerless in their spectral grip. He struggled to free himself from his invisible captors, but it was useless.

That night, folks in town noticed a light, brighter than usual, burning in the forest. The following morning, when Victor didn't return, they searched the woods.

All they found were ashes, still warm, and the scent of death.

Victor was never seen again, but on dark, moonless nights, you can still hear a wail in the wind. Locals say it's Victor's voice.

Think twice before *you* laugh at the locals, won't you?

— Ghost stories have always fascinated Sandra Yokely.
She went to Writer's Digest School and has had

*several poems and essays published. She grew up near an
Native American burial ground where she could see
lights close by in the woods—a story?*

Acknowledgements

∎

A heartfelt thank you must first go to the Town of Cornelius, the true genesis for this collection. During the research and writing of the Town's centennial history, longtime residents shared their oral histories and many of these shared a common thread — ghost stories. Only three such tales are recorded in A Town By Any Other Name, *but the other stories, shall we say, haunted Lorimer Press for the next year or so. Hence, this book.*

Writers from Charlotte, to Concord, to Winston-Salem, N.C., answered the Call for Entries, and we appreciate each and every response. The 13 stories selected cover a range of experience and showcase a depth of writing talent.

We owe a debt of gratitude to those behind the scenes who helped bring the stories to life. Some of the illustrations in this book are based on photographs supplied by the writers; others are our own invention. Meg Taylor spent a day gallivanting around the Piedmont snapping pictures that served as the basis for a majority of the illustrations. (It should be noted that Alex Sutton played the role of corpse for the art that accompanies Ghosts of Old Winston.*) Thanks to Sophie, whose image complements* Fall, *and to Sophie's handlers for their hospitality at Carolina Raptor Center. Special thanks to Amy Rogers at Novello Festival Press for sharing the blueprint for launching projects like this and to Lois Mendenhall at Parnassus Books for sharing her vast knowledge and enthusiasm.*

Thanks also to writer and friend Bill Bennett for encouraging the project over many months and for his long standing support of Lorimer Press. And, our gratitude to Dr. Robert Whitton and to Belinda Higdon.